~Don't Worry, GRANDPA~

For Audrey

A Red Fox Book

Published by Random House Children's Books
20 Vauxhall Bridge Road, London SW1V 2SA

A division of Random House UK Ltd
London Melbourne Sydney Auckland
Johannesburg and agencies throughout the world

Copyright © Nick Ward 1994

3 5 7 9 10 8 6 4 2

First published in Great Britain by Hutchinson Children's Books 1994

Red Fox edition 1998

Printed in China

RANDOM HOUSE UK Limited Reg. No. 954009

ISBN 0 09 933391 0

~Don't Worry, GRANDPA~

Nick Ward

RED FOX

Grandpa was making tea when a flurry of leaves spiralled past the window. BOOM! the sky rumbled.

'Sounds like a storm brewing,' he said to Charlie.

'Never mind, Grandpa,' replied the child. 'It's time for our story.'

Charlie climbed on Grandpa's knee and settled down to listen.

'Once upon a long, long time ago …' began Grandpa. But just then the house shook as the sky gave another, deeper rumble.

'Oh, dear,' muttered Grandpa. 'I don't like thunderstorms, Charlie. Do you?'

'Don't worry, Grandpa,' said Charlie. 'It's only the giants coming out to play.'

They slam their door and rush outside,
leaping and hollering.

'Giants, is it?' laughed Grandpa, patting
Charlie's head. 'Well, if you see one, you tell him
to get off home at once.'

　　He put a slice of bread on his toasting fork
and held it over the fire.

The sky darkened. CRA-ACK! it thundered.
   'Oh dear, it's getting nearer, Charlie,' said
Grandpa.
   'Don't worry, Grandpa,' whispered Charlie.
'It's only those giants playing marbles.'

They send huge boulders rolling and rumbling over the hills, casting their inky shadows as they play.

CRASH! Grandpa jumped as a jagged
flame split the sky.
   'My goodness,' he wailed. 'That was close.'
   'Don't worry, Grandpa,' said Charlie. 'It's
only the giants lighting their sparklers.'

The sparklers fizz into life. The giants wave them through the air, leaving tails of crackling fire.

WHOOSH! Rain began bucketing down and the wind howled across the countryside.

'Oh dear,' Grandpa exclaimed.

'Don't worry, Grandpa,' said Charlie. 'It's only the giants playing water chase.'

With buckets full to the brim, they romp after each other. Splash! Then they race away, water teeming to the ground below. Trees bend and bow as the giants charge past. The air is filled with the thunder of their footsteps. Their cheers become the wind.

Rain lashed against the window panes and the
wind whistled down the chimney. Grandpa
sighed deeply. 'I have never liked thunderstorms,
Charlie,' he said.

'Don't worry,' smiled Charlie. 'Come and have
a lie-down and get warm. I'll read the story, and
when I've finished all the giants will be gone.'
    'Giants, giants? You and your giants,' yawned
Grandpa as he dropped off to sleep.

Grandpa's bedroom window rattled in the storm. Charlie looked up. 'Shhh! Stop your noise,' he whispered to the giant. 'You'll wake my Grandpa. Get off home now.'

The giant smiled at Charlie and waved goodbye.

When Grandpa woke up the storm was gone.
The evening sun sparkled on the ground as
Grandpa and Charlie made their way outside
to finish the story.

    'Giants indeed,' said Grandpa …

'Whatever next!'

Some bestselling Red Fox picture books

THE BIG ALFIE AND ANNIE ROSE STORYBOOK
by Shirley Hughes
OLD BEAR
by Jane Hissey
OI! GET OFF OUR TRAIN
by John Burningham
DON'T DO THAT!
by Tony Ross
NOT NOW, BERNARD
by David McKee
ALL JOIN IN
by Quentin Blake
THE WHALES' SONG
by Gary Blythe and Dyan Sheldon
JESUS' CHRISTMAS PARTY
by Nicholas Allan
THE PATCHWORK CAT
by Nicola Bayley and William Mayne
WILLY AND HUGH
by Anthony Browne
THE WINTER HEDGEHOG
by Ann and Reg Cartwright
A DARK, DARK TALE
by Ruth Brown
HARRY, THE DIRTY DOG
by Gene Zion and Margaret Bloy Graham
DR XARGLE'S BOOK OF EARTHLETS
by Jeanne Willis and Tony Ross
WHERE'S THE BABY?
by Pat Hutchins